Houses
Past and Present

by Donna Watson

PEARSON

Scott
Foresman

Editorial Offices: Glenview, Illinois • Parsippany, New Jersey • New York, New York
Sales Offices: Needham, Massachusetts • Duluth, Georgia • Glenview, Illinois
Coppell, Texas • Ontario, California • Mesa, Arizona

ISBN: 0-328-13351-5

8 9 10 V0G1 14 13 12 11 10 09 08

Where do you go when there is a storm? If you're wise, you stay inside your home, school, or another building. You don't want to be stuck outside! Buildings and other shelters protect us from the weather. Everyone needs shelter.

Have you ever thought about how shelter has changed since the early years of the United States? Three hundred years ago, America was not a separate country. Instead, it was several settlements of people ruled by Great Britain. These settlements were called colonies. Because settlers lived in colonies, this period of time is known as the colonial era. The colonial era lasted until 1776. The people who came to settle here during that time were called colonists.

When the colonists arrived, there were no houses, hotels, or motels. There were no supply stores. So how did the colonists find shelter?

They built their houses by using supplies they had brought and materials from the surrounding land. There were many challenges to settling the new land. One of the biggest was making shelters before winter came.

Since the colonists arrived by ship, the ship was their home while the first houses were being built. A common house was built first to store the building tools and other supplies. The single men of the group stayed on shore in the common house to ease crowding on the ship.

As the houses were built, families left the ship and moved into them. Smaller families shared houses until enough houses were built for each family to have its own.

Colonists came to the New World
on sailing ships like this one.

The colonists chopped down trees from nearby forests to build their homes. Although they used clay to fill in the spaces between the logs, their houses were often very drafty. This was because the colonists had a difficult time finding logs of equal size and fitting them together in exactly the right way.

The colonists built homes similar to the homes they were used to. Many of these early homes had thatched roofs, which were common in England. **Thatch** is straw or leaves that have been gathered and bundled together to be used as a roof or covering.

Early colonial houses were small, wooden structures with thatched roofs and wooden chimneys.

NEW ENGLAND

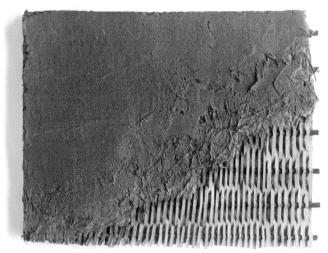

Wattle and daub between the braces formed the walls of the first settlers' homes.

As colonial life in America progressed, people learned to build better homes. Supports called cross braces made the houses stronger. Less wind, dust, rain, and snow entered the houses because the spaces between the braces were now filled in with a combination of wattle and daub. **Wattle** is the name given to twigs and sticks that are woven together. **Daub** is a mixture of clay, straw, and water. The wattle and daub were a big improvement over the clay used earlier.

The first colonial chimneys were usually made of wood and lined with clay. As soon as the colonists were able to make chimneys out of bricks or stones, they switched to using those building materials. Chimneys made out of bricks and stones are far safer than wooden ones, which could catch fire easily.

The Swedish and Finnish colonists of Delaware built the first true log cabins in America. By this time the colonists had learned that carving the logs at both ends allowed them to fit together much better. Moss, leaves, and mud were stuffed between the logs to keep out the cold and wind.

Window openings were covered with oiled paper. This paper let in some light. Often, a blanket would be hung in the doorway because doors were difficult to make at that time.

Log cabin roofs usually were covered with bark or large wooden shingles called shakes. Roofs were sloped so that snow would slide down and off. Chimneys and fireplaces were often made of rocks and stones. The fireplaces were used for heating the home and cooking.

The beams on the ceiling of this home fit together.

Settlers fastened the logs together with wooden pegs that they made by hand. Before blacksmiths were common in the colonies, nails had to be shipped from Europe. Later, blacksmiths shaped nails and hinges so that doors and cabinets could be hung.

When people couldn't pay for a blacksmith, they were able to hang doors by attaching them to walls with leather straps. In this case, latchstrings were used to open the doors.

This area was used for cooking and eating.

Most early colonial homes were simple, rectangular-shaped buildings that measured about sixteen feet long and fourteen feet wide. Many had a loft in the top with a small ladder that was attached to the floor. Several children could sleep in the loft, which was also used as a storage space.

The family area surrounded the fireplace. Early colonial fireplaces were much bigger than they are today. In cold weather, wood burned all day in order to warm up the cabin. Colonists had to constantly check the fireplaces to make sure that the fires did not go out. Without lighters and reliable matches, it could be very difficult to restart a fire in the colonial era!

By the beginning of the 1700s, colonial homes had developed very differently for different kinds of colonists.

People who lived near the wilderness still had small log cabins. Farmers often had larger log houses. Log farmhouses were built with squared-off logs that fit well together. The roof was usually made of cut logs or bark shingles.

By that time, people had learned how to build homes without using any nails or pegs. They first cut a rectangular hole, called a **mortise,** in one piece of wood. Then they cut a **tenon,** or a piece that sticks out from the main section, in the connecting piece of wood. When they put the tenon into the mortise, the pieces of wood stayed together.

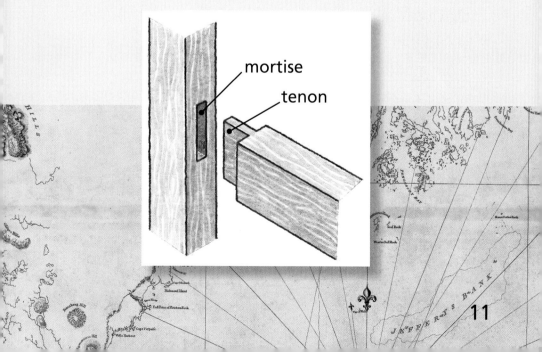

mortise

tenon

These squared-log houses were also popular with colonists who lived in cities, although other people in cities had houses made of planks or bricks. Planks, or boards, were created by cutting squared-off logs into long, thin pieces.

This plank house has a shake shingle roof.

By the 1700s, wealthier people had begun to live in brick houses. These houses required much work to build. Before building, bricks had to be made. This was done by taking clay from riverbanks and mixing it with water in a pug mill. A **pug mill** was a hollow tub that contained a shaft with knives sticking out of it.

When the clay was placed in the mill, it was mixed or ground until it was fine. Then it was mashed into a thick paste and put into rectangular wooden frames that had been dampened in water and dipped in sand so that the clay wouldn't stick to the frame. The bricks were dried for several weeks before being placed in hot ovens, called **kilns,** to bake and harden. Only then could building begin on the brick house.

Building a brick house involved a lot of work.

The insides of colonial houses were more comfortable by this time. Floors were made of smooth planks, clay, or puncheons. A **puncheon** floor was made by laying down half-logs with the flat side up.

Thick, swirled glass filled the windows of colonial homes of that time. The glass let light in, but people could not see through the glass to the outside. Wealthy colonists could order sash windows from England if they wanted the kind of windows that could slide open.

Of course, electricity wasn't an everyday part of colonial life as it is in modern America. Homes were lit with sunlight or candlelight. The candles were usually made by the women of the family, who used **tallow,** another name for animal fat.

Since candles were often burned for light, most roofs in larger towns or cities were no longer made of thatch. Thatch caught fire too easily. Instead, roofs were usually made of shake shingles or tiles. In some areas, such as Vermont, a type of rock called slate was used for roofing.

A chandelier of candles lights a room for dancing.

15

During the pioneer era of the 1800s, settlers moved west to the prairie lands. There were no forests of tall trees to cut down for lumber. They built their first homes with a different material than colonial settlers had used.

These settlers found a way to use the ground itself to make their first homes. All around them was the grass of the prairie. The grass had deep roots that held the dirt below it.

Pioneer families used plows to cut through the grass-covered ground, or sod. With a plow they were able to dig the grass up in long strips. Then they cut the strips of sod into sections.

The pieces of sod were stacked like bricks to build the walls of the shelter. The roof was made of willow brush and covered with sod. The insides of the walls were sometimes covered with mud or clay and painted white.

Although there were many insects and much dirt to sweep, these homes were sturdy. They lasted until the settlers could have lumber shipped to them to build a log cabin.

Section of sod

The pioneers who moved west built their first homes out of sod.

The colonists and pioneers worked hard to build their homes. These days, very few Americans build their own homes. Instead, most people hire building contractors, who build homes for them. Others buy homes that have already been built.

Today's homes can be covered with materials such as vinyl, aluminum, steel, brick, stone, logs, or adobe. Modern roofs are made of materials that prevent fire.

Almost all of today's homes have more than one room, with some homes having several bedrooms, bathrooms, living areas, and other spaces. Many homes have garages attached.

Candles are still common in many homes in the United States today. However, most people today don't use them as their main source of lighting. Instead, candles are used for decoration, or for emergency lighting when the electric lights lose power.

Today's homes often have many windows. They are covered with glass that lets light in but keeps snow, rain, and wind out.

Although many homes today have fireplaces, they're usually smaller. Instead of using fireplaces for heat, today's homes are warmed by modern furnaces. That same system may also provide air conditioning during hot summer days.

Swedish and Finnish settlers built America's first true log cabins.

An English-style cottage

Today's homes are very different from those of colonial or pioneer times. But they give people the shelter that they need, just as homes from the earlier days did.

Modern building methods allow people to live in homes that have many more comforts than houses of long ago. Yet in places such as New England, many people still live happily in homes that were built hundreds of years ago! Wherever you live, it's a good bet that there are many different kinds of homes all around you. Now that you've learned more about building materials, take a tour of your neighborhood and see how the houses are made!

This house is framed with metal.

Homes Change

You have read about many of the changes in the ways that houses in America have been built. Now, on separate sheets of drawing paper, draw pictures of each major style of house.

You should draw five separate pictures in all. The first will show what early colonists built. For the second picture, draw a house showing the improvements of the middle colonial years. For the third picture, make a drawing that shows a home of one of the wealthier colonists. The fourth picture will be of an early pioneer home. The last one should be of a modern home.

Feel free to use books and the Internet to help you get your drawings just right!

If classroom materials are available, work together in small groups to create a model of one of the houses described in the book. Assign one person to collect the materials, someone else to handle the glue, and another person to cut out the shapes and assemble them.

When your group has completed the drawings and models, get together with other groups to compare them. Using this book and the outside sources that you have found, discuss how each group drew the houses and created the models.

Glossary

daub *n.* a coating or covering of plaster, clay, mud, or any other sticky material.

kilns *n.* very hot ovens, usually used for making bricks or pottery.

mortise *n.* a hole in one piece of wood cut to receive the tenon or another piece so as to form a joint.

pug mill *n.* a hollow tub with knives in it used for mixing and grinding clay into bricks.

puncheon *n.* a type of flooring in which halved logs are laid with the flat sides turned up.

tallow *n.* animal fat used to make soap and candles.

tenon *n.* the end of a piece of wood cut so as to fit into the mortise in another piece and so form a joint.

thatch *n.* straw or palm leaves used as a roof or covering.

wattle *n.* sticks interwoven with twigs and branches.